Bears Out There

by Joanne Ryder   illustrated by Jo Ellen McAllister-Stammen

ATHENEUM
BOOKS FOR YOUNG READERS

Atheneum Books for Young Readers
An imprint of Simon & Schuster Children's Publishing Division
1230 Avenue of the Americas
New York, NY 10022

The text of this book is set in Bookman Light.
The illustrations are rendered in colored pencil.

Printed in the United States of America

10 9 8 7 6 5 4 3 2 1

Library of Congress Cataloging-in-Publication Data
Ryder, Joanne.
Bears out there / by Joanne Ryder. —1st ed.
p.   cm.
Summary: Snug in the comfort of his home, a boy imagines
the woods full of bears that eat and play and watch the night come, just as he does.
ISBN 0–689–31780–8
[1. Bears—Fiction. 2. Imagination—Fiction.]   I. Title.
PZ7.R9752Bk   1995
[E]—dc20   91–39802

To Gretchen Staas,
who feels the animals around her

—J. R.

To my son Timothy, who loves bears

—J. M. S.

There are bears out there.
I can feel them.

Asleep in the woods
bears curl, soft and dark.
Tucked under branches
that droop from tall trees,
there are big bears,
yawning and blinking
and stretching—
like me.

There are bears
waking early
while the day
is still gray,
shaking soft dirt
and old leaves
from their coat.
Bears wrapped in fur,
as I'm wrapped in covers,
feel the coolness of morning,
hear the wind in the trees.

There are bears out there,
sniffing the air,
sniffing the ground,
looking for food—
tender grass, tasty roots.
Hungry bears
sniff and listen
and follow a humming
that leads them
to sweetness.
Bears in the woods
eat breakfast too,
licking their paws
full of honey.

There are paths
in the woods,
paths without names
bears know by heart,
dusty trails covered
with pawprints
big and wide.
Bears have their paths
from here to there,
and I have mine.

Along these paths,
there are bears
moving slowly,
reaching high,
touching a branch
they could not
touch before.
They are tall bears,
growing taller,
growing stronger—
just like me.

Down by the water,
hot, dusty bears
wade and splash.
Large bears catch fish
with quick, strong jaws.
And dark bears, wet bears,
paddle upstream,
making long ripples
as they glide
through the coolness.
Ahhhh!

In patches of sun,
there are bears,
shaggy wet bears,
shaking sprays of water
from their thick fur.
Closing their eyes,
damp bears feel
the bright sun
all around them
as it dries them
and warms them—
like me.

In the middle of day,
bears shuffle slow,
some finding a place
to rest and be quiet.
There are bears,
in the heat of the day,
sitting in cool mud,
lying in soft grass,
and sleeping
within shady trees,
dreaming dreams
of their own,
all alone.

In the tall grass,
young bears are hiding,
tumbling and wrestling.
Their mama is watching,
keeping them safe,
calling them softly
or growling a warning.

Woof, woof.
Danger is coming!
Small bears dash
to the closest of trees.
Their sharp claws
cling to bark
as they climb.
Tucked in the branches,
bears hide in shadows
until Mama calls,
and they run to her side.

She leads them to bushes
drooping with berries.
There are bears out there,
eating and eating
till their pink tongues
turn dark.
I can feel them,
sticky-faced bears,
fat and full
of sweetness.

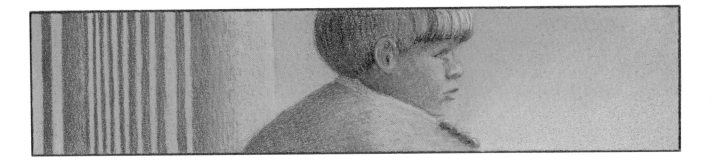

Deep in the woods,
there are bears,
sipping from streams,
nibbling thin leaves,
rubbing their backs
against trees just to scratch.
Hungry bears, sleepy bears,
feel the coolness of evening,
watch the world turning dark—
just like me.

Under the moon,
there are flat-footed bears
walking softly,
quietly through the night.
I sit on our porch
looking at stars and
feeling the bears,
dark in the dark woods.
I am glad
there are bears out there.
I am glad
I can feel them.

The screen door thumps and clicks
as Papa comes to find me.
"What are you looking at?" he asks.
"Just the night," I tell him.
"There are bears out there, Papa."
"Uh-hmm," he says.
And we stand in the porchlight,
side by side, watching, listening,
feeling the bears that roam,
that belong in the deep, dark woods.

Author's Note

Black bears (*Ursus americanus*) live in the forests and swamps of North America. Their fur may be black, brown, or cinnamon in color. Black bears use their excellent sense of smell and fine hearing to find food. Omnivores, they eat whatever is available—plants, roots, berries, nuts, insects, fish, and small animals. When bears find a bee tree, they will eat the honey, honeycomb, and bee larvae. Bears hunt alone but meet where food is abundant—in places such as a hillside covered with bushes of ripe berries.

Though black bears explore slowly, they are powerful animals who can run quickly, swim far, and climb well. They may be active any time of the day or night. Unless disturbed by people, they are more often active in twilight and daylight than at night.

Cubs—usually two—are born in the winter and may stay with their mother for more than a year. She nurses and protects them, and teaches them how and where to find food.

Generations of bears make their own deeply rutted trails to favored eating grounds. Bears leave other marks in the forest too. They may scratch against a tree and leave tufts of molting fur or reach high to claw the bark, possibly as a territorial sign.

When people develop, live near, or visit wilderness areas, they come into contact with black bears. Curious bears quickly learn that garbage dumps, feeders, livestock, and campsites are easy sources of food. It is dangerous for bears to depend on people for food.

Black bears are wild animals. They need places where they can live protected and undisturbed. Then there will always be bears out there.